D1537810

Reading Beauty

Kimberly Long Cockroft

Illustrated by **Mary Grace Corpus**

To Avery:
Reading is Rad!

—Mary Grace
Corpus

PELICAN PUBLISHING COMPANY

GRETNA 2018

The word "Pelican" and the depiction of a pelican are trademarks of Pelican Publishing Company, Inc., and are registered in the U.S. Patent and Trademark Office.

Library of Congress Cataloging-in-Publication Data

Names: Cockroft, Kimberly Long, author. | Corpus, Mary Grace, illustrator.
Title: Reading Beauty / by Kimberly Long Cockroft ; illustrated by Mary Grace Corpus.
Description: Gretna : Pelican Publishing Company, 2018. | Summary: Gabe and Ellie both hate to read, but when the school librarian, Ms. Molly, causes Ellie to fall into a deep read, only a fellow book-hater can save her.
Identifiers: LCCN 2017034722| ISBN 9781455623594 (hardcover : alk. paper) ISBN 9781455623600 (ebook)
Subjects: | CYAC: Books and reading—Fiction. | Libraries—Fiction. | Blessing and cursing—Fiction. | Best friends—Fiction. | Friendship—Fiction. | Schools—Fiction.
Classification: LCC PZ7.1.C632 Re 2018 | DDC [E]-dc23 LC record available at https://lccn.loc.gov/2017034722

Printed in Malaysia
Published by Pelican Publishing Company, Inc.
1000 Burmaster Street, Gretna, Louisiana 70053

To my three reading beauties: M, E, and B

Ellie and Gabe liked a lot of things. They liked to make art out of their lunches. They liked soccer. They liked turtles. And they *loved* to chew gum. They wanted to break Moose School's record for Biggest Bubble.

But they did not like reading. Not one bit.

Library was the worst. Ms. Molly said, "Pick a book and read quietly."

Ellie and Gabe hid under Pip. They unwrapped a new pack of gum.

Suddenly, Pip's leaves parted. Eyes big as moons stared at them.

"There you are," Ms. Molly said. "Why aren't you reading?"

Ellie popped a piece of gum in her mouth. Then she said three fateful words:

"Reading is BORING."

Pip shivered. Pip shook. Pip's leaves covered Ms. Molly's head like green snakes. Ms. Molly grew tall and terrible. Thunder rumbled. Ellie grabbed Gabe's hand. They hid their eyes.

"Ellie, listen closely," Ms. Molly roared. "In sixteen minutes, you will cut your finger on the page of a book. Then you will fall into a *deep read* for all of eternity! AH, HA, HA, HA, HA!"

Then everything was back to normal. Pip shrunk back into a tame potted plant. Ms. Molly smiled. Had it really happened? "By the way, no gum in the library," Ms. Molly said. Gabe and Ellie threw away their gum. They sat at a table with two books.

In no time, Ellie fell asleep. When the bell rang
for lunch, she jumped. A page of her book cut her
finger. "Ouch!" she said. "Paper cut!" Blood beaded
on her fingertip.

"Lunchtime," called Gabe. "Come on, Ellie!"

"Hmm," Ellie said. "Interesting!" She turned a page of her book, *How Octopuses Eat*.

"Are you . . . *reading?*" Gabe gasped.

"Did you know that octopuses can eat sharks?" Ellie said.

"Um, no," Gabe said, "but I've got a salami sandwich to eat."

Ellie did not come to lunch or recess. On the way home, she almost walked into a tree. A week passed. Ellie read while she ate. She read through her favorite TV shows. She even read in the shower. She read about lizards, wild flowers, and skydiving. She learned how to build a snow cave.

"Wow," Ellie said. She closed a book about dragons. "Reading is WONDERFUL."

"Want to ride bikes this afternoon?" Gabe asked.

"Sorry. I'm reading *The Jungle Book*," Ellie said. "I'm at the part with the tiger. I have to find out what happens next."

"Want to chew gum? I've got a new kind—grape-kiwi!"
But Ellie was already deep into another book. Gabe
walked away sadly. He did not think reading was fun. It
made his head hurt. It had taken away his best friend!
"Reading STINKS!" he groaned.

One day after school, Ellie did not go home. She took a big bowl of apples into the library. Then she lay down under Pip and read. She would not stop. Next morning, no one could see her. Books blocked the door.

The principal of Moose School shouted. The mayor gave a speech. The news truck came. The whole town stood at the door of the library.

"Come out!" they cried. Someone heard a page turn. Someone heard an apple crunch. But Ellie would not come out. She was in a DEEP READ.

"I will never see my best friend again!" Gabe wailed.

Ms. Molly calmly sipped her tea. "There is one way to break the spell," she said. "A person who HATES reading must read a book from beginning to end. But it can't be just any reading. It must be a *read of true love*."

"Oh, dear." The principal shook her head. "The spell will never be broken. Everyone at Moose School LOVES to read."

"Not everyone," Ms. Molly said.
"Me?" Gabe yelped. "Never! I'll save Ellie on my own. Step back, everyone. I'm going in!"

Before him rose mountains of books, stacked high and deep.

It was a wild journey. Wolves and witches snarled from picture book covers. A tower of board books fell on his head. But he fought on. He had to free his best friend!

Gabe slid down a hill of magazines.
Ah! There she was at last!

"Ellie!" Gabe shouted.

Ellie held up one more book. It was the last book in the library.

"Ellie, can you hear me?"

Ellie opened the book. "STOP READING!" Gabe cried. Ellie licked a finger. She turned the first page.

"I'm here to save you!" Gabe shouted. But it was no use.

Gabe walked closer. He would grab Ellie's book and run. The spell would be broken!

Suddenly Gabe stopped. He stared at Ellie's book. Then he read the title: *How to Blow the Biggest Bubble in the World.* Ellie turned a page. "Move over," Gabe said.

Night came. Gabe did not come back. Everyone at Moose School was worried. "Call the fire department!" shouted the mayor.

But then Ms. Molly said, "Listen!" They heard the crashing of books. Then . . .

"Hello!" Ellie said. "Boy, am I hungry!"
Everyone cheered.

"Hey, Ms. Molly, can I check this book
out?" Gabe waved a book with a bright
red cover. "I'd like to read it again."

Gabe read his book six times. Then he blew the biggest bubble Moose School had ever seen!

These days, Gabe and Ellie like a lot of things. They like worms. They like drums. They like gum, of course. And they LOVE to read. Most days, you can find them lying under Pip, with their noses in books.

So was the spell broken? Only Ms. Molly and Pip know, and they're not saying.

Author's Note

Of all the places I have walked into, libraries must be the most magical. Have you ever opened the cover of a book and wondered what you would find inside? Where you would go? Whom you would meet? A story has the power to send you back in time or into the future, to transport you to other lands and kingdoms. I've met ogres, talking rabbits, and some of my best friends in the pages of books.

Librarians might just have the best jobs ever. With each library card they hand out, they offer a ticket to strange and marvelous worlds. Open a book and, like Reading Beauty, you might fall under a spell—the magic of a *deep read*. But chances are, unlike the Sleeping Beauty of the original fairy tale, you will never want the spell to be broken.